To Ken, Kenny, and Richard, who bring magic to my life! –L.M.

STERLING CHILDREN'S BOOKS
New York

An Imprint of Sterling Publishing
1166 Avenue of the Americas
New York, NY 10036

ISBN 978-1-4549-1602-4

Distributed in Canada by Sterling Publishing
c/o Canadian Manda Group, 664 Annette Street
Toronto, Ontario, Canada M6S 2C8
Distributed in the United Kingdom by GMC Distribution Services
Castle Place, 166 High Street, Lewes, East Sussex, England BN7 1XU
Distributed in Australia by Capricorn Link (Australia) Pty. Ltd.
P.O. Box 704, Windsor, NSW 2756, Australia

For information about custom editions, special sales, and premium and corporate
purchases, please contact Sterling Special Sales at 800-805-5489 or specialsales@
sterlingpublishing.com.

Manufactured in China
Lot #:
2 4 6 8 10 9 7 5 3 1
05/15

www.sterlingpublishing.com/kids

HideAway Hedgehog

and the
Magical Rainbow

A HideAway Pets Book

by Lisa McCue

STERLING CHILDREN'S BOOKS
New York

One beautiful day, peeking out from her hole
Mama hedgehog decided to take a short stroll.

But for mama-to-be this was no time to stray
for her litter of hoglets was due on this day.

The roses were blooming, the sky was bright blue.
Mama thought, "I'll stay out just a minute or two."

But once in the sun, with the trees and the flowers,
that "minute or two" quickly turned into hours!

She watched bees buzzing by,
and nibbled on clover.

When she came to a stream,
Mama tiptoed right over.

She was picking some berries that grew down the lane . . .

. . . when a dark cloud rolled in and it started to rain.

Wind whipped through the trees. Bright lightning flashed.
And then came the thunder, which rumbled and crashed!

"I must find a shelter," she thought with alarm.
"If I don't, then my babies may come to great harm."

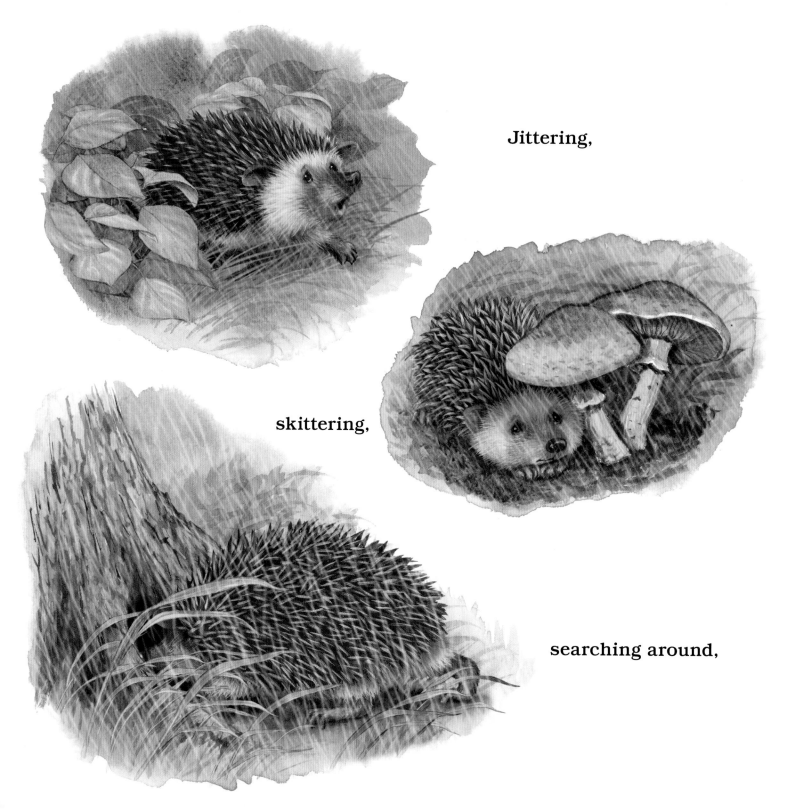

Jittering,

skittering,

searching around,

Mama hedgehog discovered a pot on the ground.

Taking shelter inside, Mama shivered in fear—
for the time to deliver her babies was near!

The thunderstorm raged. Lightning bolts lit the skies.
Safe inside, frightened Mama did not realize . . .

that the pot she was in, all tarnished and old,
was really a magical pot made of gold!

When the storm rolled away, Mama noticed a change.

As the sun rays peeked out, she could feel something strange.

The pot flashed and sparkled, and started to glow.

Colors swirled around Mama—then made a rainbow!

As each of the rainbow's bright colors took form,
into this world a new hoglet was born!

Yellow

Orange

Red

Green

Blue

Indigo

Violet

It's mentioned in legends, both new ones and old,

that finding a rainbow's remote pot of gold

means good luck is magically granted to you.

Now each Rainbow Hedgehog is magical, too!

Ruby brings passion and love where she goes.

When **Clementine's** near, creativity flows.

Sunny spreads laughter and joy all around.

With **Clover** nearby, health and peace can be found.

Honest and loyal is **Jay's** shade of blue.

Indie has strength and is really smart, too.

Violet is different—a dreamer, unique.

But . . .

Mama's love is the magic
that everyone seeks.